TALES OF A
LOST KINGDOM

Jordio bashen, hase parian mulkoten baghatae.
E. L.

First American Edition published in 2007 by
Enchanted Lion Books, 45 Main Street, Suite 519, Brooklyn, NY 11201

Originally published in French as *Contes d'un royaume perdu*
Text and Illustrations © Editions Gallimard Jeunesse, 2003

Photographs for travelog © Yannik L'Homme
Translation © 2007 by Enchanted Lion Books

[A CIP record is on file with the Library of Congress]

ISBN-10: 1-59270-072-1
ISBN-13: 978-1-59270-072-1

Printed in Hong Kong

2 4 6 8 10 9 7 5 3 1

TALES OF A LOST KINGDOM

A Journey into Northwest Pakistan

Written by Erik L'Homme
Illustrated by François Place

Translated by Claudia Zoe Bedrick

Stories collected by the author in the kingdom of Chitral
at the border between Pakistan and Afghanistan

ENCHANTED LION BOOKS
New York

NANO BEGAL
Begal's Mother

Chitral is a country at the end of the world, a near-forgotten country of wild valleys surrounded by immense mountains.

Behind these mountains are high, desolate plateaus and a sky so deep that it would be easy to think of it as the place where clouds go to die when they have grown too old.

The rivers that run through Chitral are dark and turbulent. The winds that blow carry smells that are both harsh and intoxicating.

In Chitral, time passes more severely and more gently than elsewhere.

The men risk their lives on unstable mountainsides when looking for wood or bringing their goats to pasture. The women wear themselves out working in the fields. And yet, these hard-working people manage to retain their humor and to smile.

The men choose with care the flower that they place in their caps each day. The women quarrel gaily while making up their eyes with kohl. And all of them tell stories or sing while drinking tea and eating rounds of flat bread. Above all else, however, their greatest pleasure is to watch the polo players confront each other on the meadow near the village when spring arrives.

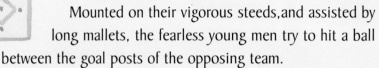

Mounted on their vigorous steeds, and assisted by long mallets, the fearless young men try to hit a ball between the goal posts of the opposing team.

According to the elders, the game rouses the good weather to return.

Every evening the men, women, and children crowd around the edge of the field to see the teams compete with skill and daring.

Musicians are always there and their joyful melodies carry peoples' hearts along after the rough wooden balls.

In one of Chitral's lush green valleys, surrounded by high, dry mountains, the village of Shoghor can be found.

It is a typical village, such as are scattered throughout the kingdom. The houses are built of earth and wood with only a single room for eating, sleeping, and talking around the fire. It is there that the whole family gathers.

In Chitral, the family is most important of all.

Three centuries ago, the captain of the polo team of Shoghor was named Begal. He was a young man, both strong and courageous, who handled his wooden mallet better than anyone. His eyes were as limpid as the spring from which the girls drew water. His hair was as light as the wheat reaped by the women once it had ripened.

His horse, Bumburush*, was the fastest horse of all. With his gray-white coat drenched with sweat and his nostrils flaring, he would run after the ball without Begal having to spur him on.

The other players were proud to count Begal among them. The previous season they had won against all of the other villages of the kingdom!

* A Chitrali word that means "Thunder."

So it came as no surprise when one fine spring day the king of Chitral, who also played polo, set out for Shoghor from his palace in Birmoghlasht, accompanied by a number of courtiers.

As soon as the king arrived in Shoghor, he was invited to the home of the village leader, who served him the finest foods he had to offer: thick bread and cheese, boiled goat's meat sprinkled with hot butter and fresh mulberries.

When tea had been served with lots of milk and sugar, as was the custom for important visitors, the king revealed his intentions:

— I have come to challenge Begal to a polo match!

The news traveled through the village like the sound of a gun shot. Soon it reached the ears of Begal who lived alone with his

mother in a small house at the edge of the village.

— This is good, came his reply. Tomorrow I will defeat the king and I will become the greatest polo player in the whole kingdom.

Begal's mother did not share his enthusiasm. Many years before she had lost her husband to a terrible fall in the mountains. She had suffered enough in her life to recognize unhappiness when it announced itself.

— The king is cunning and cruel. Be suspicious of him! He will not forgive you if you win.

But his mother's warnings did not keep Begal from sleeping happily and dreaming of glory.

The next day on the grounds where the match was to be held, a great crowd gathered, made up of the inhabitants of neighboring hamlets who had come to see Begal and the king compete.

When the king and his men advanced on their richly harnessed mounts, there were murmurs of admiration. But when Begal and his companions appeared in their turn, these murmurs turned into shouts of joy.

The horsemen faced each other. The royal team was arrayed in tunics of white wool embroidered with silver. The players of Shoghor wore the same dirty, old clothes they wore every day.

— Entry for the king! called out the village leader, whose duty it was to referee.

Begal did not protest. The visiting team always went first. The king threw his horse into a gallop. Having reached the middle of the field, he tossed the ball into the air. Whirling his mallet around, he hit the ball violently, sending it far out in front. Spurred on by Begal, Bumburush threw himself into immediate pursuit, taking off in a cloud of dust.

As the game allows, a player can be rough as long

as he is not brutal, and so Begal moved against the king, preventing him from hitting the ball anew. The king flew into a fit of rage. He tried to shake off the captain who kept obstructing him, but wherever he found himself, Begal too was there. As the end of the round approached, still nobody had succeeded in scoring.

At that moment, the ball was on the royal side, with Bumburush protecting it from the other mallets with his legs. This enabled Begal to recover it easily, and with complete calm he hit the ball through the goal posts. The village of Shoghor erupted with shouts of joy. Begal had carried his team to victory!

— I demand a rematch for tomorrow, snarled the horribly ill-tempered king, who had just refused to shake hands with the victor.

Begal agreed to the king's demand. It made no difference to him to have to carry his victory into the field again! He would triumph as many times as was necessary to have the king recognize his worth.

Evening came and Begal's mother was uneasy. Night, populated by demons, had fallen, and nobody dared risk remaining outside!

But Begal had not returned home yet.

A courageous woman, Begal's mother took a flaming log from the fire to light her way, armed herself with a knife, and went out in search of her son.

She found him at the side of the road that ran through the village. He was stretched out and appeared to be sleeping. Full of apprehension, she approached him, trembling.

Kneeling down, she shook him, but he did not move. It was then that she noticed a reddish tear in his shirt near to his heart. Heaving with sobs, she collapsed on top of him.

— My son! My Begal! the unhappy woman cried out. Didn't I tell you to be on your guard against the king? Didn't I warn you of his wickedness and his cruelty?

Once her tears had dried, she picked herself up, draped Begal across her back and took the road home.

The next day, people came in even greater number and from even farther away for the rematch that would pit the king's team against Begal's. The king's players showed themselves first. They were

dressed in green tunics embroidered with gold. The crowd whispered in wonder.

When the players of Shoghor approached exclamations of surprise could be heard. At their head, mounted on Bumburush, was Begal, dressed in black, with his face concealed behind a scarf.

The king and his companions went white. The villagers, however, took this extravagance as a provocation of the king for having refused to accept his defeat, and they applauded Begal.

The village chief announced:

— Entry for Begal!

The pale king kept his eyes fixed on the masked captain.

Begal engaged the ball with his usual dexterity and galloped after it. A second well-placed hit of the ball sent it between the opposing goal posts. The villagers, looking to each other, began to chant:

— Be-gal! Be-gal!

Begal scored another three points before the signal that indicated the end of the game was given. The royal team had lost for a second time.

Begal rode toward the king. The entire crowd held its breath, thinking that Begal would oblige the king to shake his hand and to acknowledge his victory!

But Begal stopped his horse several feet away from the king and slowly unwound his scarf.

An uproar of shock and surprise ensued: it was not Begal who was mounted on Bumburush! It was his mother! Begal's mother had defeated the king!

With a piercing look, her eyes bore into those of the king, and in a voice loud enough that everyone could hear her, she addressed him:

— King! Why did you kill my son? He was happy, and so gentle! He bit into life as if into a crunchy apple! He shined in the night of my old age! King! Why did you kill him? Today an old woman has defeated you, so it was not Begal who was too strong, but you who are too weak! It was not that he was too skillful, but that you are too inept! If you had wished, my Begal would have helped you to become better. But you preferred to cut down the tree that put you in its shade than to attempt to push up higher than it! You may very well be king, but you are worth no more than the most stupid of idiots.

Having said these words, she turned her back and returned home to tend to the body of her son.

It is told that the king lowered his head and blushed deep crimson. It further is told that he had a richly embroidered coat brought to Begal's mother to serve as the shroud for her unhappy son. Finally it is told that the king never dared to set foot in Shoghor again, and that he exempted the village from taxes thereafter. Should we believe this? Mothers often have more honor than kings!

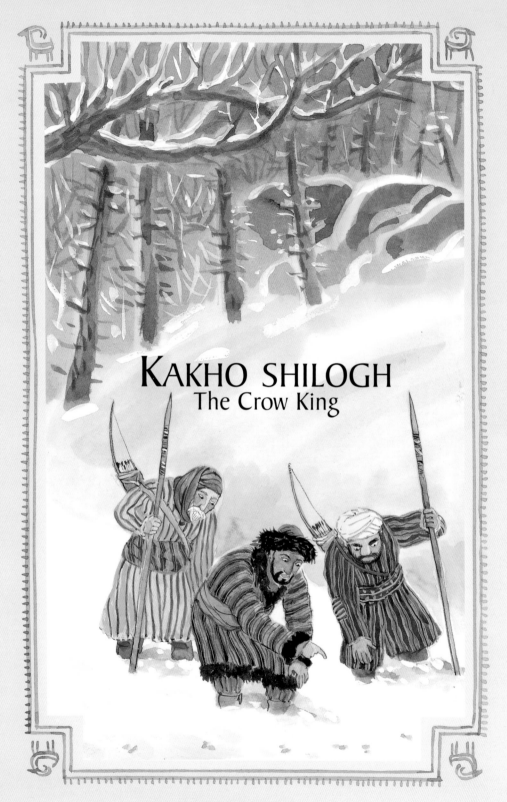

KAKHO SHILOGH
The Crow King

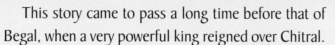

This story came to pass a long time before that of Begal, when a very powerful king reigned over Chitral. But, as powerful as he might have been, today nobody remembers his real name! He is remembered only as the Crow King, a name that was given to him after a certain adventure.

More than anything, this king was passionate about hunting. Outfitted with bow and spear, he loved to go on horseback from one end of his kingdom to the other and to track the swiftest beasts through the mountains.

He was not a mean man. He simply liked to put his strength and skill to the test. As the peasants murmured among themselves, the time that he spent hunting was time he couldn't squander on harassing them or in going to war.

No, the greatest fault of this king, and of many kings elsewhere, was his pride. And his was limitless. He was a man who was as big and as strong as a bear, and he imagined himself to be the most powerful of all terrestrial kings!

One day, the king set out to hunt the snow leopard in a distant part of the kingdom, then called Wershigum. He brought three companions with him, who also were the best hunters in the country: Gech, who could see further than any other; Kar, who could hear better than any other; and Niskar, who could smell better than any other.

Over a long stretch of time, the king and his hunters followed the trail of an animal that did not want to let itself be captured. Feeling tired and ill humored about losing the scent of the animal, the king admitted his wish to take a rest.

— My king, I see a tree under which you might stretch out, said Ghech.

The king assented and they walked over to the tree. It was a giant cedar whose branches extended from one end of the valley to the other. Its trunk was so large that the

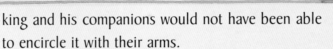

king and his companions would not have been able
to encircle it with their arms.

— It's a good place to rest, agreed the king, who sat down and leaned back against the tree with all his force.

When his robust back pressed against the trunk, the cedar shook.

— Did you see that? bragged the king. I am so strong that I can shake the strongest tree in the kingdom simply by pressing back against it!

He was no longer angry at the animal that had made him run such a long way.

— You are as big as a bear, my king, said Ghech.

— You are as strong as a leopard, my king, said Kar

— You are as noble as a falcon, my king, said Niskar.

The king accepted these compliments from his hunters with a grin.

— It is true! I am big, I am strong, I am…

But he could not finish his sentence, for a crow that sat perched on a branch above him had just relieved himself onto the royal head.

The king flew into a terrible rage.

— Crow! What have you dared to do? You will regret it! Come down and you will see!

But the crow merely threw a scornful look at the king, who was attempting to clean up his forehead with an embroidered hand-kerchief.

— Ghech! Kar! Niskar! Catch that bird for me.

The three hunters went into action, grabbing into the tree. But the crow didn't wait for them and flew off cawing. At that moment, the men turned around with a questioning look to the king.

— Ghech! Kar! Niskar! No matter what it takes, bring me back
    that bird!

    The three hunters, used to obeying, took their

leave and ran after the crow, which flew straight
ahead of them, stopping here and there in order to
rest. They ran for a long, long time.

At times, they would lose the crow from view. Then Ghech
would look around and exclaim:

— He's over there! I see him!

When night fell and Ghech could no longer see anything, Kar
would prick up his ears.

— He is over there! I hear him.

In the early morning when a thick fog would settle around them
and Kar could no longer hear anything, then Niskar would sniff loudly.

— He is there! I can smell him!

Moving from valleys to peaks, they finally arrived in the valley of
Owir, which lay stretched out sleepily at the foot of Tirich Mir, the
sacred mountains in whose heights the fairies dwell. The three hunters
were completely exhausted, as was the crow, which flapped its wings
and flew heavily in zigzags, stopping on the roof of each house.

Ghech, Kar and Niskar passed in front of a miserable hut at the
side of the road, from which an old woman hailed
them.

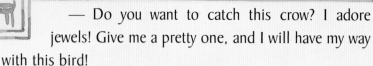

— Do you want to catch this crow? I adore jewels! Give me a pretty one, and I will have my way with this bird!

The hunters willingly accepted the old woman's offer. Ghech dug into his pants' pocket and found nothing. Kar slid his hand into the pocket of his shirt and brought out a handful of dried apricots.

Niskar took a deep breath and drew out from his vest the jewel he had counted on giving to his wife when he returned home. It was a beautiful blue stone set into a disk of engraved cooper. The old woman clapped her hands delightedly.

— A thing promised is a thing owed! Come into my house and rest while I catch your bird.

The hunters did not have to be persuaded. They settled themselves on stools, ate flat bread with good appetite, and gulped down the bowl of milk that their hostess brought them.

While they regained their energy, the old woman killed a sheep, gutted it, and unrolled and cleaned its intestines. In this way she was able to obtain a long, nearly invisible tube.

Having done this, she filled a bowl with fruits for which crows have a tremendous fondness. In the middle of the fruit she concealed one end of the sheep gut, and she placed the bowl in the road.

Finally, keeping the other end of gut in her hand, she hid herself inside the house.

— What are you playing at old woman? exclaimed Ghech with surprise.

— Your crow must be as hungry as you were before having met me, she replied mysteriously.

Indeed, the crow felt horribly hungry.

When he saw the plate filled with good things sitting in the middle of the road, he couldn't resist and threw himself at it.

And so what was meant to arrive, arrived. By stuffing his beak, the crow soon swallowed the little bit of intestine hidden in the bowl. When that happened, the old woman began to blow furiously with all her might into the other end of the tube. The crow began to swell up with air and grew so swollen that he was unable to fly! The hunters caught him without difficulty,

trapping him under a bird net.

Happy to have brought their pursuit to an end, the three men retraced their steps back to Wershigum, the tree, and their king, though not before having warmly thanked the clever little old woman. When they returned into the valley, the king awaited them, pacing a hundred steps back and forth under the great cedar. His anger had not diminished in the least.

Hence, when he caught sight of the imprisoned crow, he let out a triumphant shout.

— Brave hunters! You caught that insolent bird! And you, unhappy crow, you will pay for your deed!

He seized the net and brought the crow close to his face.

— Look at me! Now do you not feel remorse for having sullied the head of the most powerful of kings?

Once again the crow turned a scornful eye upon the king.

— Dig at the foot of this tree, at just the place where you were sitting, said the crow.

The men looked at the crow with surprise. The king, more curious than annoyed, ordered the hunters to do as the crow asked.

So Ghech, Kar and Niskar dug at the foot of the immense tree. Soon they found a strange object.

At first they took it to be a crown, but then they saw that it was a ring, a very ancient ring, and such a big one that each of their heads could pass right through it!

With the object unearthed, the crow spoke:

— Long ago this ring belonged to a king who in his time had no equal. Look at his size! Imagine a man who could wear that on his finger. If such a man could not hold on to his throne beyond earthly life, how can you, so much less strong, feel proud merely for having made a tree tremble? In relieving myself on your head, it is humility that I wished for you to remember!

From sheer surprise, the king dropped the net he was holding to the ground. Taking advantage of this to escape, the crow flew off emitting caws that sounded very much like laughter.

It is told that the king lowered his head and blushed deep crimson. It also is told that he had the fantastic jewel found at the foot of the tree brought to the old woman who had aided in the capture of the crow, and thereby had allowed this lesson to be learned. Finally, it is told that the king ceased to hunt and that he forbade the throwing of stones at crows. Should we believe this? Crows are often wiser than kings!

HASHIM BIGIM
The Disappointed Princess

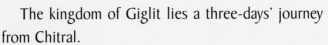

The kingdom of Giglit lies a three-days' journey from Chitral.

To get there, it is first necessary to ascend the steep Shandur pass, then to cross a plateau covered with dark-water lakes, and finally to travel along the length of a capricious river.

A long, long time ago, between the period of the Crow King and that of Begal, a very beautiful princess named Hashim Bigim lived in Giglet.

She was so beautiful that all of the men who saw her were sobered into melancholy. So terribly beautiful that a poet even put out his eyes in order to preserve her face as the last image he ever saw! Indeed, she was so remarkably beautiful that numerous princes, some very handsome and others very rich, came from great distances to visit her and to ask for her hand in marriage.

But her father, the king of Giglit, had other plans.

— Hashim Bigim, my daughter, you will marry the son of the king of Chitral, our neighbor.

The two kings wished to strengthen the ties between their two kingdoms by uniting their children. The princess, who trusted her father, responded favorably.

Satisfied, the king of Chitral agreed to prepare for festivities at his palace. With snow blocking the Shandur pass until the beginning of summer, the nuptials were set for the month of July.

But it was still only May.

The palace of the king of Gilgit bore more resemblance to a regular house than to a large manor or estate. Built of earth and wood like all of the houses in the village, it was simply larger and better situated than the others. Armed men stood guard, and a garden full of magnificent flowers surrounded it.

In ordinary times Hashim Bigim's maturity, despite her youth and lack of experience, won her admiration from all of those inside the palace. But thoughts of her impending marriage made her as restless and impatient as a child.

— Oh, Gul Naz, what a hurry I am in to meet my future husband! the princess confided to her servant.

As Gul Naz was the same age as her mistress, she was able to understand just how she felt.

— He is surely very strong and very handsome, elaborated Gul Naz.

— Yes! Hashim Bigim exclaimed. He cannot be otherwise. If my father sent away so many handsome young men, it must be because the one he has chosen surpasses them all!

The princess returned to her mirror, which had been given to her by her father. He had purchased it from a merchant from Sind who was on his way to China. Hashim Bigim contemplated her own image while Gul Naz brushed her hair.

— Will he find me to his taste? she asked, suddenly anxious. Will I be beautiful enough for him?

— You are the most beautiful girl in the two kingdoms, her servant reassured her.

Restless, the princess got up from the stool on which she had been sitting, left her rug-covered room and went out into the garden to smell the roses.

— Oh, Gul Naz, she began again, my future husband is surely a very courageous man! He has surely won a number of battles!

— He also must be as generous as he is brave and as gentle as he is strong, added her servant.

At these words, the princess twirled around in circles, thinking life wonderful.

And thus the days separating May from June passed.

But Gul Naz, who came and went in the palace and through the streets of the village, heard a terrible rumor. It was murmured, albeit in innuendoes to keep word from reaching the ears of the princess, that the prince of Chitral was far from being as handsome and brave as she, unfortunately, was in the midst of imagining.

The servant, who loved her mistress dearly, grew sad and downcast. How deceptive and disappointing if the princess's future spouse was not the one for whom she wished, and the prince of Chitral was revealed to be just as rumor had him!

And so Gul Naz ceased to encourage the enthusiasm of her mistress for this man upon whom she had never set eyes.

— Oh, Gul Naz, how I long to meet my future husband! the princess continued to confide as Gul Naz combed her hair.

— It isn't good to be impatient, came Gul Naz's reply. And of course, she continued, to leave a father for a husband is simply to change masters.

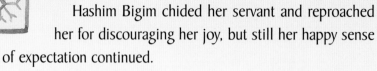

Hashim Bigim chided her servant and reproached her for discouraging her joy, but still her happy sense of expectation continued.

— Oh, Gul Naz, she again exclaimed while skipping in the garden, I believe that I will be able to spend my days listening to my husband recount his exploits!

— He who talks too much, doesn't do anything, replied Gul Naz.

Hashim Bigim again reproached her servant for her sadness and her unkind words.

And thus the days separating June from July passed.

At last the moment for setting out on the road to Chitral arrived. Gul Naz had not succeeded in discouraging Hashim Bigim, who continued to rejoice with the same ardor for marriage even now that it was near.

The king of Gilgit had succeeded in forming an impressive caravan: donkeys and mules were saddled with gifts that the princess would offer as dowery to the prince of Chitral while the members of the royal family, the guards and the guests went off on horseback.

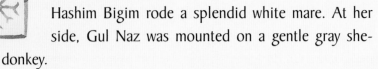

Hashim Bigim rode a splendid white mare. At her side, Gul Naz was mounted on a gentle gray she-donkey.

—At last! confided the princess to Gul Naz on the first day of their trip. At last I am going to meet my friend!

Gul Naz didn't say anything and sadly lowered her eyes.

— I do not understand you, the exasperated princess replied. One might say it does not give you pleasure to see me happy!

— It's the river, responded Gul Naz. The din that it makes gives me a headache.

On the second day, Hashim Bigim said to her servant:

—Gul Naz, I feel my heart fluttering at the thought that I will see my prince shortly!

Gul Naz raised her face toward the sky and her eyes filled with tears.

— You are impossible, sighed the princess. Now you are crying at my happiness.

— It's the lakes, murmured Gul Naz. They are so black and seem so deep that I am afraid.

On the third day, Hashim Bigim approached Gul Naz and whispered:

— Gul Naz, my faithful servant, my friend, I believe I am afraid.

Gul Naz took Hashim Bigim affectionately in her arms.

— Hashim Bigim, be courageous: a princess you are and a princess you will remain.

At last the caravan approached the palace, which reared up, majestic, on the banks of the river that the melting snows had transformed into a raging torrent. The king of Chitral and his courtiers awaited the king of Giglit and his entourage on the far side of the bridge that allowed the coursing waters to be crossed.

— Is he there? whispered Hashim Bigim who had closed her eyes.

Gul Naz did not reply.

— Do you see him? she asked once again.

Gul Naz remained silent.

— What does he look like? she finally asked.

Gul Naz began to cry, and Hashim Bigim resolved to look for herself. On the other bank, at the king's side, a man sat fidgeting in his saddle, flailing his arms.

The princess let out a cry of despair, which she stifled in her throat. Her eyes, now wide, stared at the prince that her father had chosen as her spouse. He was a dwarf, deformed and grimacing. Drool dribbled down his chin and he seemed to grunt in the manner of a beast.

The princess turned toward her servant with the face of one completely lost. She let several tears roll down her cheeks, but dried them quickly with the back of her hand.

— Gul Naz…You are the only one with the ability to understand me, and the only one that I regret losing! Forgive me!

Departing suddenly from the caravan, deaf to the cries of her father and those of her servant, Hashim Bigim spurred her mare in the direction of the torrent. The

animal hesitated for just a moment before the dark and raging waters, before yielding to the princess's firm spur. Together they disappeared into the violent current.

It is told that the two kings lowered their heads and blushed deep crimson. It also is told that Hashim Bigim's father adopted Gul Naz and treated her as if she were his own daughter. Finally it is told that in both Chitral and Gilgit children were no longer obliged to marry against their wishes. Should we believe this? The soul of a princess is often more pure than that of kings!

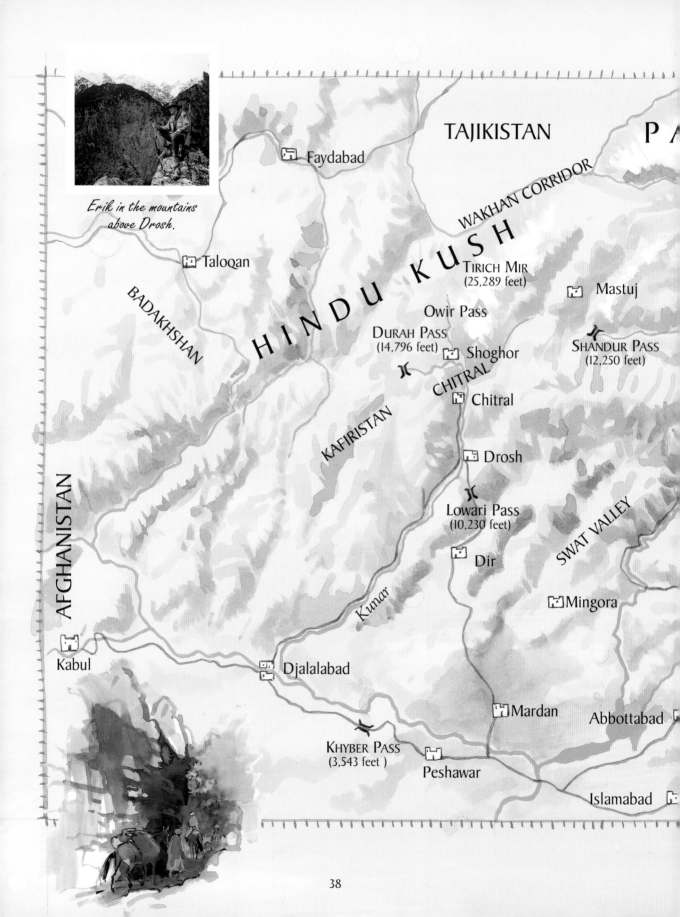

Erik in the mountains
above Drosh.

TAJIKISTAN

P A

WAKHAN CORRIDOR

Faydabad

H I N D U   K U S H

BADAKHSHAN

Taloqan

TIRICH MIR
(25,289 feet)

Mastuj

Owir Pass

DURAH PASS
(14,796 feet)

Shoghor

SHANDUR PASS
(12,250 feet)

CHITRAL

Chitral

KAFIRISTAN

Drosh

Lowari Pass
(10,230 feet)

SWAT VALLEY

AFGHANISTAN

Dir

Kunar

Mingora

Kabul

Djalalabad

Mardan

Abbottabad

KHYBER PASS
(3,543 feet)

Peshawar

Islamabad

MIR

Valley River

KHUNJERAB PASS
(15,420 feet)

BOROGHIL PASS
(12,392 feet)

ARSHIGUM

HUNZA
RIVER

Yasin

Baltit

Gilgit

RAKAPOSHI
(25,551 feet)

Gilgit

Indus

NANGA PARBAT
(26,778 feet)

KARAKORAM

BALTISTAN

CHINA

K2
(28,251 feet)

Indus

HIMALAYAS

INDIA

*Yannik and Jordi with Prince Hilal
and his entourage in the Owir Valley.*

*The ranges of the Hindu Kush, Karakoram and the Himalayas
at the confluence of the Giglit and Indus rivers.*

*Shahi, Chitral's grand mosque
(20th century)*

39

"I learned to know and to love the ancient kingdom of Chitral (found in the Northwest Province of Pakistan, bordering Afghanistan) by exploring it from one end to the other. My brother, Yannik, and a friend, Jordi, accompanied me. We stayed in Chitral for eleven months in 1990 and for ten months in 1994, during which time we lived through many incredible adventures. Over that period, I also was able to learn Khowar, the language of our hosts. It is because of this knowledge that I was able to gather the stories collected in this volume during a final stay of two months in the spring of 1998.

Erik and Jordi in the hamlet of Dop, in the valley of Shishikuh

"The north of Pakistan, stark and beautiful, immediately comes to mind as the place where men, titans and gods meet. This is how I can best describe the mountainous region that stretches between the ranges of the Hindu Kush, Karakoram and the Himalayas. Here the numerous valleys, often as many kingdoms, are situated at an altitude of 3,200—16,500 feet! Facing these immense mountains, one has the feeling of having arrived at the doors of our world.

Bus tickets assure connection between Mingora-Kalam and Pindi-Peshawar.

40

"The trip up into the mountains always begins with the sounds of the town, of cars, of horns and of people shouting. Then, very quickly, once the bags have been loaded on to the roof of an old jeep, the adventure begins! The road turns into a trail along which herds in transhumance move, along with traditional trucks covered with decorations that serve as talismans against evil spirits. After a while, beyond the tribal zones occupied by the fierce and unsociable Pashtuns -- zones where customs have the force of law, the Lowari pass is reached. Closed by snow from November to June, this is the great door into the kingdom of Chitral.

A truck decorated to keep evil at bay.

"Chitral, capital of the district of the same name, can be found in the middle of the largest valley, situated on both sides of an icy stream and existing under the severe gaze of the surrounding mountains. Its great mosque, with the peak of Tirich Mir in the background, seems to come straight out of an English novel of a century ago. The men who wander through the bizarre with black or blonde beards, light or dark eyes, often wear a flower, symbolizing the peaceful character of the Chitrali, stuck in their caps.

Erik's notebook with jottings on the Chitrali language

41

"From December to March the entire district, excluding the central part of the valley to the south, is under snow. What this means is that each village lives at a slower pace, relying upon only itself. Calmed by the crackling of flames in hearth or stove, all live according to the rhythm of the stories that the men and women tell their children. Even the mountains, beautiful for the wolves and the leopards, grow gentle under their blankets of white.

The mountain hamlet of Kanderi in the north-east of Drosh.

"At the end of winter, life resumes its normal course. With long beards, skin reddened by the cold, and their feet wrapped in strips of cloth, the men ascend the steep and seemingly infinite slopes to cut wood, after which they sit amidst their sheep watching vultures glide across the sky. The women tend to the cows and the sheep, helping to sooth the newborn animals, work in the fields, and prepare meals as they listen to the birds outside chirp the promise of spring.

As always, the Chitrali still work their fields with a swing-plow.

A young Chitrali wearing his
Pakistani schoolboy's cap.

"It is the beginning of summer. The sky's lucidity comes as a summons from the north, from those limitless spaces where the clouds certainly must melt away.

"At the foot of Tirich Mir, the sacred mountain where the fairies live, lies the valley of Owir, which is where Begal's mother confronted the terrible king and the sly old woman captured the insolent crow. The road carries us along despite ourselves, sloping down as we go, skirting off in the direction of Borogol and Wershigum. At times, the teasing laughter of a child can be heard, coming as a surprise or a question. Above the horizon and unattainable, the sky seems to have been painted by the hand of a god. Further on even still, there are other infinities, so pure that the air of the mountains and the water of the lakes challenge our very idea of them.

Yannik on the road from Borogol.

43

Chitrali children on the road
from Mastyi.

Musicians from Surnay who accompany all of the polo matches.

"At an altitude of 12,250 feet lies the Shandur pass, mid-way on a three-day's trip of rambling roads that link Chitral and Gilgit. This is the same route that was taken several centuries ago by Princess Hashim Bigim and led her to her tragic encounter. Each year since a very long time ago, the best polo players of the two ancient kingdoms have confronted each other here before the impassioned gaze of thousands of men and women.

"Who today remembers that this game, played here for centuries and perhaps even born in this region, previously had the value of a rite, symbolizing the conflict between bad and good weather, the harsh and the gentle seasons. Mingling English traditions and marking a half-century of British presence in the district, as well as

Polo players face off at the Shandur Pass.

millenarian emotions, the rough confrontations on this high plateau elicit impassioned shouts and carry the spirit away.

"Among the large tents that are raised up at the time of a tournament, everyone finds their own way to eat and sleep. Dancing and music fill the evenings around a hundred fires under the stars. For us, as visitors, there is something of a good bye in the sorrowful songs—a good bye to these proud and skillful people of the North.

"It is prince Abdul Ghan Khan who told me the story of the Crow King. This nobleman of Kesu is a giant with a gray beard who took a liking to me and often wished to have me around. He was also a great hunter, and I remember an extraordinary hunting party in which he included me: six days during

Prince Abdul Ghani Khan of Kesu.

which we walked a lot, practiced our skill by taking aim at rocks, and…never saw an animal! In the spring of 1998, comfortably settled in his garden, the prince punctuated his telling of a favorite story with bursts of laughter in which the three or four people present willingly joined.

While constantly refilling my cup with milk tea and sugar, a drink for which the Chitrali have a great fondness, he repeated with infinite patience the passages that I had difficulty grasping. At the end of this process, happy to have confirmed my real and lively interest in his old story from legendary times, he proudly drew me into a big hug.

Chitrali dancers wearing traditional coats and wool caps.

"One afternoon I had the opportunity to assist at one of the first polo matches of the season, held on grounds in the town of Chitral. I was in the company of Farid Ahmad, a student friend. Funny and cultured, Farid had two reasons for being unhappy: he loved polo, but was a pitiful horseman; and he loved music, but didn't know how to play any. To laugh at himself, he confessed that his favorite song happened to be Nano Begal, a song that recounts the story of a celebrated polo match that took place in the 17th century under the reign of the evil Katour dynasty. To tease him, I asked him to sing it to me. He raised the stakes, and the outcome was that he would help me transcribe the words of the song. Later, in order to give me a better idea of the story, he invited me to his home for an unforgettable evening that brought together the sitar players Sultan Ghani and Mahmad Ali and the singer, Ghairet ud-Din.

Farid Ahmad having lunch with his younger brothers in the region of Shoghor.

"Before departing, I asked Farid about the poignant melody that brought the evening to a close and moved all who were there. It was a song that I had heard back in 1990, played at the

home of Prince Abdul by the celebrated sitar player of Koghuz, Mastan Khan. In reply, Farid told me about Hashim Bigim, whose tragic story actually took place at the end of the XIV century, at the beginning of the glorious dynasty of the Rais. I took this story down in my notebook with great care.

Sitar player in Mastuj.

Fast food in the bazaar, Chitral style.

"Certainly there are a multitude of other stories that exist in the oral tradition of Chitral. But few in the West understand Khowar, the language of the Chitrali, as I do, and among the stories that I've been able to collect, some are too poetic, while others are too far from our manner of thinking to be truly understood and appreciated.

"So it happens that three stories remain—*Nano Begal, Kakho Shilogh*, and *Hashim Bigim*, all celebrated in Chitral, but unknown to us until now. In telling these stories, I have taken liberties of recreation in order to make them more accessible than they otherwise would be. Indeed, no Chitrali would expect anything else since according to their traditions stories are always enriched by the personality of each teller.

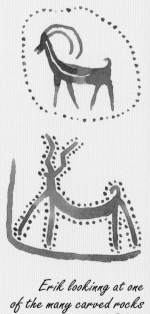

Erik lookinng at one of the many carved rocks in the region of Gilgit.